Dewey's Magical Sleigh

Santa

By Brahm Wenger & Alan Green   Illustrated by Jean Gillmore

The Helpful Doo-its

Dewey Doo-it   Howie Doo-it   Anita Doo-it   Kenya Doo-it   Willie Doo-it   Woody Doo-it

Dedicated to Larry and Frances Jones who turned one of life's interruptions into an opportunity to feed hungry children throughout the world.

Special thanks to Lord & Taylor without whose support *Dewey's Magical Sleigh* would never fly.
Thanks also to Lori Freedlander Wenger, Laurel Green, Ken and Pam Everson, Chuck and Heidi Glauser,
Brendan Nguyen and Nicholas and Adam Wenger for helping develop this special Christmas story.

Library of Congress Control Number: 2005932016   ISBN Number: 0-9745143-6-5
Dewey Doo-it and Dewey he Helpful Doo-it are registered trademarks of The Helpful Doo-its Project, LLC
Published by RandallFraser Publishing, 2082 Business Center Drive, Suite 163, Irvine, CA 92612, 866-339-3999
www.DeweyDooit.com. Printed in the United States

Once upon a time, not too long ago,
The Doo-its found a deer lying weak in the snow.
"Howie," said Dewey, "let's look in your pack.
Let's give him some food. This deer needs a snack!"

Soon the young deer was back on his feet.
"Thank you. I just needed something to eat."
What the Doo-its didn't see as they waved their good-byes
Was that this little deer flew up into the sky!

Then, suddenly who should appear 'round the bend,
But ol' Santa Claus and their new *reindeer* friend.
"Would you like to be elves?" Santa asked with a smile.
"I've been watching you Doo-its for quite a long while."

"You see, for my elves I choose only the best.
By helping my reindeer you all passed the test!"
Well, of course they said, "Yes" and climbed up on the sleigh.
They were laughing with glee as they heard Santa say...

"Come Dewey and Howie! Bundle up, it's chilly.
Come Kenya, Anita and Woody and Willie.
Up over the treetops and mountaintops high,
Up – all the way up – to the North Pole we'll fly!"

The next day, when Dewey had toys to repair,
He noticed nearby the young elf Taylor Bear.
He was sitting alone, and to Dewey's surprise,
He was reading a letter with tears in his eyes.

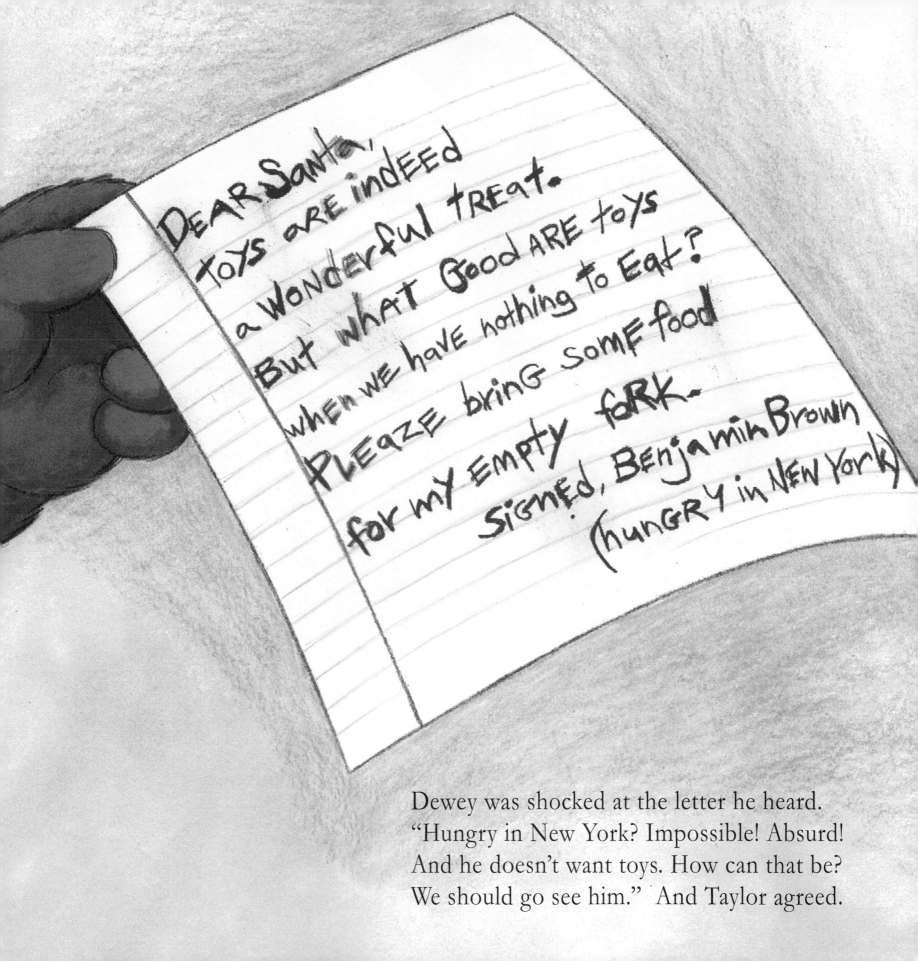

Dewey was shocked at the letter he heard.
"Hungry in New York? Impossible! Absurd!
And he doesn't want toys. How can that be?
We should go see him." And Taylor agreed.

After finishing work and laying their tools down,
They raced to New York to see Benjamin Brown.
But just as they reached toward the doorbell to ring,
They saw in the alley a very strange thing.

"Someone is going through the trash," Dewey said.
"Who is that little bear holding some bread?
He's taking old food that others threw out
And filling his pockets. What's that all about?"

Soon the small bear trudged away in the snow.
"Let's follow," said Taylor, "and see where he goes."
Curiously they watched, as the bear turned around
And walked into the house of one Benjamin Brown.

"That must be Benjamin," said Dewey. "Oh my!
"And that must be his family," Taylor Bear cried.
Then, quietly creeping down the dark alley way,
They peeked in the window and heard Benjamin say…

"Here's a sandwich I found in an old paper sack,
And some uneaten apples that someone threw back.
Here are some crackers and an orange for Mother,
And a carton of milk for our new baby brother."

They watched as the Brown family gathered around
And ate the food slowly, not making a sound.
"They don't need toys. They need *food*!" Dewey said.
"We must go tell Santa." So off the two sped.

"Santa, here's a most unusual note.
It's from Benjamin Brown - you must hear what he wrote.
He doesn't want toys or new games to play,
He only wants food on this Christmas day."

"Food?" Santa said, stroking his beard,
"We only make toys and games around here.
Anyway, 'tis the night before Christmas and all through the shop,
The elves are all working. There's no time to stop."

The Doo-its were sad eating dinner that night.
Sad until Dewey cried, "Stop! It's not right!
Let's wrap up this meal, there's plenty to share
And take it to Benjamin to show him we care."

"And we'll add Christmas cheer for the whole family Brown!
We'll transform Santa's workshop (when the elves aren't around)
Into a wondrous new place to make sweet, yummy treats
To make Benjamin's Christmas meal fun and complete."

Howie Doo-it baked cookies. Anita made pies.
Kenya decorated gingerbread men...with gumdrops for eyes.
Woody Doo-it made donuts with cinnamon swirls
And Willie made popcorn balls for good boys and girls.

They rushed to Santa with their goodies and frills
But his bag was already quite stuffed to the gills.
"I know what we need! Follow me," Santa said.
"The answer lies hidden and stored in my shed."

"Here's my very first sleigh. It's like an old friend.
And now we have reason to use it again.
So load up the food – let's go!" Santa cried,
"For on this Christmas Eve we have *two* sleighs to fly!"

"But who," Taylor asked, "will fly sleigh number two?"
Santa firmly declared, "Little Dewey, that's who!
For tonight we'll feed the children in a special new way
With our gift to the world...*Dewey's Magical Sleigh!*"

While Santa put toys 'neath the old Christmas tree,
Dewey laid out the food for the Brown family.
They were done in a flash and soon back in the air.
More children were waiting – they had no time to spare.

When the long night gave way to a bright winter dawn
They flew back to look in on young Benjamin Brown.
The Browns were aglow as they feasted and played
And joy came to all on that great Christmas day.

Now every December the Doo-its come help
(For Santa has made them officially elves.)
Dewey and Taylor Bear make their own list
So that no hungry child will ever be missed.

And this Holiday Season, when the year sees its end,
Look out for ol' Santa and his special new friend.
'Cause on this Christmas Eve you might hear a child say,
"I think I just saw **Dewey's Magical Sleigh!**"

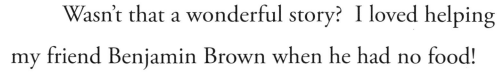

Happy Holidays Everyone!

Wasn't that a wonderful story? I loved helping my friend Benjamin Brown when he had no food!

Dewey's Magical Sleigh was inspired by another person who helps children who are hungry. His name is Larry Jones. Almost 27 years ago Larry Jones met a hungry boy just like Benjamin. He helped that little boy get the food he urgently needed and made up his mind to help hungry children everywhere. But because there are so many hungry children – millions of them – Larry and his wife Frances created *Feed The Children*. Word spread to others who wanted to help feed hungry children too. Today *Feed The Children* is helping millions of boys and girls in the United States and around the world get the good food they need.

You and your family can help a hungry child right now! Just $7 will provide 50 pounds of good nutritious food for one hungry child's family for two weeks! $14 will provide 100 pounds of food, enough for two families! You can make a gift online by visiting our website at www.HelpDewey.com, or by calling 1-800-844-6990. Or you can send a check to *Feed The Children*, P.O. Box 1, Oklahoma City, OK 73101.

Thanks, **Dewey**

Larry Jones,
Feed The Children